READER

JE
Hillert, Margaret.
It's spring, dear Dragon

MID-CONTINENT PUBLIC LIBRARY
Liberty Branch
1000 Kent Street
Liberty, MO 64068

LI

D1313609

WITHDRAWN
FROM THE RECORDS OF THE
MID-CONTINENT PUBLIC LIBRARY

A Beginning-to-Read Book

It's Spring, Dear Dragon

by Margaret Hillert
Illustrated by David Schimmell

NORWOOD HOUSE PRESS

DEAR CAREGIVER,

The *Beginning-to-Read* series is a carefully written collection of classic readers you may remember from your own childhood. Each book features text comprised of common sight words to provide your child ample practice reading the words that appear most frequently in written text. The many additional details in the pictures enhance the story and offer the opportunity for you to help your child expand oral language and develop comprehension.

Begin by reading the story to your child, followed by letting him or her read familiar words and soon your child will be able to read the story independently. At each step of the way, be sure to praise your reader's efforts to build his or her confidence as an independent reader. Discuss the pictures and encourage your child to make connections between the story and his or her own life. At the end of the story, you will find reading activities and a word list that will help your child practice and strengthen beginning reading skills.

Above all, the most important part of the reading experience is to have fun and enjoy it!

Shannon Cannon

Shannon Cannon,
Literacy Consultant

Norwood House Press • P.O. Box 316598 • Chicago, Illinois 60631
For more information about Norwood House Press please visit our website at *www.norwoodhousepress.com* or call 866-565-2900.

Text copyright ©2010 by Margaret Hillert. Illustrations and cover design copyright ©2010 by Norwood House Press, Inc. All rights reserved. No part of this book may be reproduced or utilized in any form or by any means without written permission from the publisher.

LIBRARY OF CONGRESS CATALOGING-IN-PUBLICATION DATA
    Hillert, Margaret.
    It's spring, dear dragon / by Margaret Hillert ; illustrated by David Schimmell.
       p. cm. — (A beginning-to-read book)
    Summary: "A boy and his pet dragon enjoy a spring day by playing outside and exploring all the season has to offer"--Provided by publisher.
    ISBN-13: 978-1-59953-312-4 (lib. ed. : alk. paper)
    ISBN-10: 1-59953-312-X (lib. ed. : alk. paper) [1. Dragons--Fiction. 2. Spring--Fiction.] I. Schimmell, David, ill. II. Title. III. Title: It is spring, dear Dragon.
    PZ7.H558Itq 2009
    [E]--dc22
                                                   2009003882

Manufactured in the United States of America

MID-CONTINENT PUBLIC LIBRARY - QU

3 0003 00434246 3

MID-CONTINENT PUBLIC LIBRARY
Liberty Branch
1000 Kent Street
Liberty, MO 64068

LI

Oh, no!
Look at the rain.
This is not good.
We cannot go out now.

3

You cannot go out
but this is good.
Look out here.

The little green things
will get big and pretty.
You will see.

Like this, Mother?
Like this?

8

Yes, that is good.
Now see what I have for you—
funny green hats and green cookies.

Oh, boy.
This is so good.
You are a good mother.

Oh, oh.
Look out there now.
Look way, way up.
How pretty the
rainbow is.

Now we can go out.
It will be good to see friends.

Do this.
Do this.
Jump, jump, jump.
What fun!

What is this?
How do you play this?
It looks like fun.

Oh, I see.
I can make the red one go out.

The girls are good at that.
I want to do it.

Oh, oh.
I guess I am not so good at this.

Look at that.
It is good to see that.
It makes me happy.

See what it eats.
It is good for him
but not for me!

And look here.
What a pretty bunny.
It can run and jump!

Will it come to my house?
Will it have something for me?

Oh, oh.
We have to go.
Run, run, run.

Here you are with me.
And here I am with you.
What a good friend you are, dear dragon.

The following activities support the findings of the National Reading Panel that determined the most effective components for reading instruction are: Phonemic Awareness, Phonics, Vocabulary, Fluency, and Text Comprehension.

Phonemic Awareness: The /spr/ and /str/ consonant blends

1. Say the word spring and ask your child to repeat the /**spr**/ sound.
2. Say the word string and ask your child to repeat the /**str**/ sound.
3. Explain to your child that you are going to say some words and you would like her/him to show you one finger if the sound in the word is /**spr**/ as in spring or two fingers if the sound in the word is /**str**/, as in string.

spray	strap	spree	sprint	stream
straw	spruce	strange	stripe	sprinkle

Phonics: Consonant clusters spr- and str-

1. Demonstrate how to form the letters **spr** and **str** for your child.
2. Have your child practice writing **spr** and **str** at least three times each.
3. Divide a piece of paper in half by folding it the long way. Draw a line on the fold. Turn it so that the paper has two columns. Write the words spring and string at the top of the columns.
4. Write the words above on separate index cards. Ask your child to sort the words based on the **spr** and **str** spellings.

Word Work: ABC Order

1. Ask your child to recite the alphabet. Write the letters of the alphabet on a piece of paper and sing the alphabet song together while pointing at the letters.
2. Write the following words on separate index cards: am, and, are, be, big, boy, can, cookies, cupcake, for, friend, funny, girls, green, guess, happy, hat, have, like, little, look, man, me, mother, pit, play, pretty, see,

some, spring, that, there, thing, we, what, will.

3. Place the words am, big, can, hat, look, man, play, see, that, will (mix up the order) in front of your child. Ask your child to name the first letter in each word.

4. Tell your child that you are going to work together to put the words in alphabetical order by looking at the first letter in each word. Help your child put the words in order.

5. Next, put the words for, friend, funny (mix up the order) in front of your child.

6. Tell your child that when words begin with the same letter, we put them in order based on the second letter. Help your child put the words in alphabetical order.

7. Sort the cards based on the first letter. Shuffle them and put them in piles, faced down. Have your child practice putting the words from each group in alphabetical order.

8. Challenge: Shuffle all the cards together and ask your child to put all of the words in alphabetical order.

Fluency: Shared Reading

1. Reread the story to your child at least two more times while your child tracks the print by running a finger under the words as they are read. Ask your child to read the words he or she knows with you.

2. Reread the story taking turns, alternating readers between sentences or pages of the story.

Text Comprehension: Discussion Time

1. Ask your child to retell the sequence of events in the story.

2. To check comprehension, ask your child the following questions:
   - Why couldn't the boy go outside at the beginning of the story?
   - What holiday were they celebrating with the green hats and cookies?
   - What appeared after it stopped raining?
   - What do you like to do in spring? Why?

WORD LIST

It's Spring, Dear Dragon uses the 76 words listed below.
This list can be used to practice reading the words that appear in the text.
You may wish to write the words on index cards and use them to help your
child build automatic word recognition. Regular practice with these words
will enhance your child's fluency in reading connected text.

a	dragon	here	no	that
am		him	not	the
and	eats	house	now	there
are		how		things
at	for		oh	this
	friend(s)	I	one	to
be	fun	is	out	
big	funny	it		up
boy			play	
bunny	get	jump	pretty	want
but	girls			way
	go	like	rain	we
can	good	little	rainbow	what
cannot	green	look(s)	red	will
come	guess		run	with
cookies		make(s)		
	happy	me	see	yes
dear	hats	Mother	so	you
do	have	my	something	

ABOUT THE AUTHOR Margaret Hillert has written over 80 books for children who are just learning to read. Her books have been translated into many different languages and over a million children throughout the world have read her books. She first started writing poetry as a child and has continued to write for children and adults throughout her life. A first grade teacher for 34 years, Margaret is now retired from teaching and lives in Michigan where she likes to write, take walks in the morning, and care for her three cats.

Photograph by Glenna Washburn

ABOUT THE ADVISER Shannon Cannon contributed the activities pages that appear in this book. Shannon serves as a literacy consultant and provides staff development to help improve reading instruction. She is a frequent presenter at educational conferences and workshops. Prior to this she worked as an elementary school teacher and as president of a curriculum publishing company.